"If some people really see angels, where others see empty space, let them paint the angels..."

JOHN RUSKIN

First published 2006 by Walker Books Ltd
87 Vauxhall Walk, London SE11 5HJ

2 4 6 8 10 9 7 5 3 1

© 2005 Jennifer Eachus

The right of Jennifer Eachus to be identified as
author/illustrator of this work has been asserted by her in
accordance with the Copyright, Designs and Patents Act 1988

This book has been typeset in Eva Antiqua

Printed in China

British Library Cataloguing in Publication Data: a catalogue
record for this book is available from the British Library

ISBN-13: 978-0-7445-8140-9

ISBN-10: 0-7445-8140-0

www.walkerbooks.co.uk

ANGEL

A TALE OF WONDER

✳

Jennifer Eachus

WALKER BOOKS
AND SUBSIDIARIES
LONDON · BOSTON · SYDNEY · AUCKLAND

In a corner of her garden,
Lara found a soft white feather
fallen to the earth.
"Look," she said, "a feather
from an angel."

Next she found a scrap of cloth hanging from a branch. Gold threads glistened in the sun. It's from the angel's dress, she thought.

In the morning sunshine,
beside the big old tree,
Lara saw a fox crossing
the field.

And suddenly the angel

was there!

"Will you tell me something,
Lara?" the angel asked.
Lara nodded.
"Will you tell me what
you know about wonder?"
Lara kept silent.
"Go now and find the answer."

"What is wonder?" Lara asked her father.
"Wonder," he said, "is sitting by the river
on a summer evening watching fish
among the weeds."

"What is wonder?" Lara asked her mother.
"Wonder," her mother said, "is when
the song thrush sings so sweetly from the
tree you forget the time of day."

"What is wonder?" Lara asked her brother.
"Shooting stars are wonderful," her brother said
"They whizz across the sky so fast, if you
blink for just one second they are gone."

Lara ran to tell the angel
what she had found out about
wonder — about fish, the song thrush
and the shooting stars.

The angel listened carefully.
"Those things are wonderful, it's true."
she said. "But please, Lara, tell me
something wonderful of your own."

The day had all been wonderful, Lara thought — the feather and the scrap of cloth and the fox under the big old tree. But the angel was most wonderful of all.

"Everything is wonderful," Lara said. "You make the whole world wonderful. You are my angel and you are most wonderful of all."

The angel smiled.

She spread her feathered wings

until they filled the garden.

"Thank you, Lara," she said ...

and suddenly

the angel was gone.

It was still morning in

Lara's garden.

The sun shone through

the big old tree.

And far away,

to someone else,

a soft white feather came

falling from the sky.

✳